Bubble-rific!

Adapted by Andrea Posner-Sanchez
from the script "Bubble Monkey, Blow Your Nose!" by Kent Redeker
Based on the television series created by Chris Nee
Illustrated by the Disney Storybook Art Team

 A GOLDEN BOOK · NEW YORK

randomhouse.com/kids
ISBN 978-0-7364-3236-8 (trade) — ISBN 978-0-7364-3237-5 (ebook)
Printed in the United States of America
10 9 8 7 6 5 4 3

Doc McStuffins is getting ready to head out for the day. She and her brother have been invited to a bubble-popping party.

"Come on, Doc. I wanna play with Bubble Monkey! It's gonna be a bubble-rific time! ACHOO!" Donny says as he wipes his nose on his sleeve.

Doc's mom hears all the sneezing and arrives to feel Donny's forehead. "I think you're coming down with something," she tells him. "Sorry, but I can't let you go. You'd spread your germs, and Doc, Emmie, and Alma might get sick, too."

Donny is disappointed that he won't get to play with Bubble Monkey.

When Donny's mother takes him to his room to rest, Doc touches her stethoscope. Her toys magically come to life. "Aww, I hate to see a kid denied a chance to play with a toy he loves," says Stuffy. "If only there was a way to bring the bubble party to Donny."

"Great idea!" says Doc. "I'm going to ask Emmie and Alma if I can borrow Bubble Monkey. She loves cheering kids up!"

A little while later, Doc returns home with Bubble Monkey.
She touches her stethoscope and brings the toy to life.

"It's so, so, so good to see you, Doc!" Bubble Monkey says
as she gives Doc a big hug.

Doc explains that Donny isn't feeling well and could use
some cheering up.

"I would love to help!" cries Bubble Monkey. "Yes, yes, yes!"

Doc peeks inside Donny's room. "Shh, he just fell asleep," Doc's mom says.

"I was going to see if he wanted to play with Bubble Monkey," Doc explains. "But I'll come back later."

Doc takes Bubble Monkey and her other toys to the backyard. There's Lambie, Chilly, Stuffy, Hallie, Squeakers, and Surfer Girl. Bubble Monkey is excited to see them. "Hugs, hugs, hugs! I want hugs from everyone!" she shouts.

"Bubble Monkey's sad that she didn't get to cheer up Donny," Doc says. "Now we need to cheer *her* up."

Lambie asks Bubble Monkey if she wants to wear her pink hat. "Ooh, I would love to!" replies Bubble Monkey. She models the hat for the others, but then—ACHOO! She takes the hat off and sneezes into it. When she puts it back on, it's dripping with bubble soap.

"Hey, let's play Pink Flowery Hat Tag while we're waiting for Donny to wake up," suggests Doc. "When you're 'it,' you have to wear the hat."

Bubble Monkey quickly takes the hat off and slaps it onto Stuffy's head. "You're it!" she shouts as she runs away, giggling.

Stuffy races off to tag another toy. "Come back here!"
he cries.

"No way, Dragon Dude," yells Surfer Girl as she tries
to stay out of his reach.

Then Stuffy slips. He slides right into Surfer Girl, and
they both slide into Squeakers.

The three of them slide into Lambie,
Bubble Monkey, and Chilly!

The toys can't stop! They slide into a house of blocks.

CRASH!

"You toys had one whopper of a whoopsie!" exclaims Hallie as she and Doc pull everyone out of the pile of blocks.

"I don't know what happened," says Stuffy. "My feet went all out of control."

Doc picks Stuffy up and looks at him. She rubs a finger over his tummy. "You have **soapy goo** all over you," she tells the dragon. "That's what's making you slippery and slidey."

Doc looks at the others and notices that all the toys are dripping with soap.

Then Doc turns to Bubble Monkey. "You've been sniffling and sneezing since you got here, haven't you?" she asks.

"Yeah," Bubble Monkey replies with another sniffle.

"I think you've been getting bubble soap all over everyone when you sneeze," Doc explains.

Stuffy takes the pink hat off his head and holds it up. "I think she sneezed into the hat, too."

Bubble Monkey feels awful. "I didn't mean to make everybody all slippy-slidey! I just can't stop sneezing," she admits.

Doc decides it's time for a checkup. Everyone heads to the checkup room. Hallie uses a towel to dry off the others while Doc prepares to examine Bubble Monkey.

Doc looks in Bubble Monkey's mouth and frowns. "I see a lot of bubble soap dripping into your mouth and nose," she reports. "That's what's making you sniffle and sneeze."

Then Doc places her stethoscope on Bubble Monkey's back and asks her to take a deep breath. "Hmm. I'm hearing a gurgly-gurgly sound. I'm going to need to open the panel on your back to take a look inside."

"Inside?" asks Bubble Monkey. "That sounds scary."

"We'll hold your hands to help you feel brave," offers Lambie, and Stuffy nods.

Doc gently opens the back panel. Hallie hands Doc a magnifying glass and she takes a good look.

"I see the problem!" Doc announces. "There's a tiny hole in one of your tubes. It's leaking bubble soap all over your insides. You've got a case of the Slippy-Drippys!"

"I do not like being all sniffly," says Bubble Monkey. "I do not like it at all!"

Doc gets a colorful patch and covers the hole. Then she closes the panel on Bubble Monkey's back. "Your leak is fixed."

Doc asks Bubble Monkey to blow some bubbles. She tries, but nothing comes out. "I still feel all gunky and goopy in my nose," the toy tells her sadly.

"The bubble soap leaked into your head," she tells her patient. "To clean it out, you'll have to blow your nose."

Doc gets a box of tissues and teaches Bubble Monkey how to do it.

Bubble Monkey gives a big blow.
When she's done, she throws the tissue away.
"I feel super!" she declares. "In fact, I feel bubble-riffic!"
Bubble Monkey takes a deep
breath and blows a stream of
bubbles. Doc and the toys run
around happily popping them.

"Oh, how I wish I had known
how to blow my nose in the first
place," Bubble Monkey says with
a smile. "I might have still been
sniffly, but I wouldn't have spread
my Slippy-Drippys to all my super
great friends!"

A little later, Doc and Bubble Monkey go back to Donny's room. "Look who's here," Doc says as she sets down Bubble Monkey and turns her on.

"All right! Bubble-riffic!" shouts Donny. He jumps around chasing bubbles. One lands on his nose. "It's gonna make me—ACHOO!"

Doc hands her brother a tissue. He gives a big blow and tosses the tissue in the trash. "Thanks, Doc!"

TISSUES